Moto Maki's Ghostly Mysteries
THE TIGER EYE

by Anita Yasuda
illustrated by Francesca Ficorilli

Spellbound

An Imprint of Magic Wagon
abdobooks.com

For Koji and Emi, my bookends. –AY
To Federica, for supporting me. –FF

abdobooks.com

Published by Magic Wagon, a division of ABDO, PO Box 398166, Minneapolis,
Minnesota 55439. Copyright © 2021 by Abdo Consulting Group, Inc.
International copyrights reserved in all countries. No part of this book may
be reproduced in any form without written permission from the publisher.
Spellbound™ is a trademark and logo of Magic Wagon.

Printed in the United States of America, North Mankato, Minnesota.
082020
012021

THIS BOOK CONTAINS
RECYCLED MATERIALS

Written by Anita Yasuda
Illustrated by Francesca Ficorilli
Edited by Bridget O'Brien
Art Directed by Laura Graphenteen

Library of Congress Control Number: 2019955636

Publisher's Cataloging-in-Publication Data

Names: Yasuda, Anita, author. | Ficorilli, Francesca, illustrator.
Title: The tiger eye / by Anita Yasuda ; illustrated by Francesca Ficorilli
Description: Minneapolis, Minnesota : Magic Wagon, 2021. | Series: Moto Maki's ghostly mysteries;
    book 3
Summary: Moto is excited to present his collection of lost things to his friends at the school carnival,
    but when the ghost of the tiger eye blocks him from attending the event, Moto wonders if he has
    made a colossal mistake.
Identifiers: ISBN 9781532138263 (lib. bdg.) | ISBN 9781532138980 (ebook) | ISBN 9781532139345
    (Read-to-Me ebook)
Subjects: LCSH: Ghost stories--Juvenile fiction. | Ghosts--Juvenile fiction. | Lost and found
    possessions--Juvenile fiction. | Carnivals--Juvenile fiction. | Mistakes--Juvenile fiction. | Spirit
    possession—Juvenile fiction.
Classification: DDC [FIC]--dc23

TABLE OF CONTENTS

chapter ONE
LATE FOR THE CARNIVAL

Being late for the school carnival isn't the worst thing. Missing it would be! Tonight, I'm going to let my friends in on my haunted collection. But what to show them?

Then, a twinkling bead catches my eye, and I pluck it from my desk.

"Tiger eye it is," I say and **RUSH** for the door.

In the lane, bikes stand *silently*. There are no neighbors talking or kids playing. There doesn't seem to be anyone around. Each **SHADOW** makes me freeze mid-step. I should've asked Dad to **DROP** me at school before he went to work.

Anything can happen in Ghost Month when the darkness closes in. This is when the *spirits* roam.

My friends love stories of moaning and GROANING ghosts. None of them believe those stories, but I do. I've seen all sorts of STRANGE things this week.

Just then, a **SHADOW** moves overhead, and black feathers flutter to the ground. Tiny hairs on my neck **RISE**.

I **RACE** away, pebbles fly up behind me. The sound startles the crows in a grove of trees to my left. One **SWOOPS** at my feet and tilts its head. I freeze and listen to its high-pitched scream. *CAW!*

"Beware," it seems to **SHRIEK**.

It's ridiculous to be *SCARED* of a bird, I tell myself.

But when more land, my breath QUICKENS. Their heads bob up and down. It's clear they don't want me here. I back away, one step at a time. CRASH! I've ended up toppling over a trash can.

The crows exit in one

MONSTROUS black

cloud. This is my chance to escape. I

make a SHARP turn. But where's

Timah Road?

chapter TWO

A WALL OF FOG

Instead, I bounce off a wall of fog. It feels **creepy**. When I reach out to touch it again, it won't move!

My other hand FUMBLES in my pocket for the tiger eye. Dad says the bead helps a person feel **brave**. I close my eyes and count—one, two …

Before I finish counting, a bell **RINGS**. A boy on a bike whizzes past me, and my heart skips two beats.

"Sorry," he **calls** out. "This fog appeared out of nowhere, huh?"

I nod and **SQUEEZE** the bead for more courage. As if on a pulley, the fog lifts. And I keep moving, **EAGER** to get to school.

Timah Road falls silent except for a rush of air. **WHOOSH**!
The wind tugs at laundry left to dry on poles. It whisks plastic bags upward. They *dance* like ghosts before me, when a larger movement by a sign pulls my eyes away. I almost expect a new GHOST to reveal itself!

But Vijay steps out from the

SHADOWS.

"Hold up," he says, PANTING.

"Didn't you hear me yelling?"

I sheepishly shake my head.

"You look like you've seen a

GHOST," he says.

Vijay does his best ghost

impression. He moans so loudly I think

the DEAD will rise!

"Ooooooooooooh!"

A **spook-tastic** idea hits me. To stop Vijay, I pull my tiger eye from my pocket. Its bands of orange SHINE even in the dim light.

"It's a lost thing," I whisper. "An old lady told me it was **haunted**. But it hasn't come alive—yet."

Vijay **JUMPS** back.

chapter THREE
AN ORANGE GLOW

"You brought something **haunted** to school," he says.

There's a slight *quiver* in his voice. Somewhere behind us, the crows ECHO his concern. CAW!

"I thought you weren't SCARED of *ghosts*," I say with a grin.

Vijay **SHRUGS** and hurries ahead.

"Ahh, come on," I say, holding the bead up to the sky. "It's harmless."

Vijay doesn't answer, but the tiger eye does. The stripes unfurl in a fiery swirl!

Could the old lady be right? The
tiger eye bead is **haunted**.

There's no time for me to return home. I SHOVE the bead back into my pocket. "Nothing can happen if I don't TOUCH it, right?"

Vijay shakes his head and points. An orange light shines through my pocket. It **PULSES** slow, fast, then faster.

I pull my T-shirt over my pocket, and we hurry on in silence. The air cools. In seconds, thick fog SWiRlS around us. It feels like we're in the middle of an ICY cocoon!

"What's going on?" asks Vijay.

Now it's my turn to shrug. All I know is we've got to find our way out before the fog SWALLOWS us.

I press on ever so carefully. My feet **shuffle** along the road when the smell of barbecue smoke *floats* through the air.

"The carnival's this way," I tell Vijay.

"I can walk this way blindfolded."

CRASH!

Ugh, trash cans again, and one is

STUCK to my foot!

"A walking can." Vijay SMIRKS. "Now

that's a ghost you don't see every day."

Vijay stops smiling. His **EYES**

stare over my shoulder.

"I'm not falling for that one," I say.
"You've **PRANKED** me once
already tonight."

It's not until Vijay grabs my arm
that I turn around. A spooky orange
light GLOWS through the fog.

"Tiger eye," I hear Vijay whisper.

chapter FOUR
LOST AND FOUND

My fingers reach for the tiger eye, but they come up empty. Did the bead fall out of my pocket? My stomach *dives* into a roller-coaster drop.

"The tiger eye," I tell Vijay. "It's GONE!"

Vijay narrows his eyes at me.

"Just because it's a *haunted* thing doesn't mean it's evil," I tell Vijay. "Maybe it's lost."

No sooner do I say those words than

the orange **LIGHT** fades. But there's

no time to investigate the ghost. Vijay

YANKS on my arm to go.

"Come on," he says. "The school's

over there."

The buzz of voices and the **BOOM** of drums makes me forget the ghost until a wind ROARS through the yard.

The food tents shake and tip with a *bang!* I jump. Paper lanterns spin. **WHOOSH.** The school mascot takes a tumble!

The fog *rolls* back in. It grows thicker until I can't see anything. I push and grab, but it's useless. My frustration turns to **PANIC** when I no longer hear anything either.

"Vijay, where are you?" I yell. "Anyone?"

I hold my breath as the fog **SPLITS** open.

A boy steps out. He's about my age and dressed in an **old-time** *yukata* and wooden sandals.

"Thank you," he says. "I thought I would be LOST forever."

My heart beats so **FAST**, I can't find the words to answer.

A group of kids dressed just like him appear. I **GASP**. How long have his friends been waiting for him?

The group disappears. I've got to tell
Vijay the tiger eye GHOST was a kid!
As the drums sound, I scan the yard
and I wonder. How many other spirits
*follo**wed*** me on Timah Road?

STORY NOTE

The tiger eye ghost has the characteristics of a *nurikabe*. In Japanese folk stories, a *nurikabe* is an invisible wall. The mischievous ghost blocks a person's way at night.

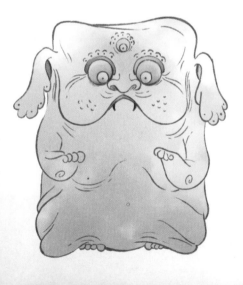

A tiger eye bead is not usually associated with GHOSTS, but with harmony and balance. So, when Moto remains **calm**, the wall of ghostly fog disappears.